SHERLOCK H
GRAPHIC MYSTER

SIR ARTHUR CONAN DOYLE'S

THE ADVENTURE OF

The Engineer's Thumb

ADAPTED BY: **Vincent Goodwin** | ILLUSTRATED BY: **Ben Dunn**

KAEDEN™

Kaeden.com
(800) 890-7323

ISBN: 978-1-63584-101-5

Title: Sherlock Holmes Graphic Mysteries: The Adventure of the Engineer's Thumb
Original novel by Sir Arthur Conan Doyle
Adapted by Vincent Goodwin
Illustrated by Ben Dunn
Colored by Robby Bevard
Lettered by Doug Dlin
Edited by Stephanie Hedlund and Rochelle Baltzer
Interior layout and design by Antarctic Press
Cover art by Ben Dunn
Cover design by Saglibene Design

Printed in Guangzhou, China
NOR/0518/CA21800517

First edition 2018

TABLE OF CONTENTS

CAST

Sherlock Holmes

Dr. John Watson

Mr. Victor Hatherly

Colonel Lysander Stark, AKA Fritz

Mystery Woman

Dr. Becher, AKA Mr. Ferguson

Inspector Bradstreet

THE ADVENTURE OF
The Engineer's Thumb

Summer 1889 at Dr. John Watson's office…

GOOD MORNING, MISTER…

…MISTER VICTOR HATHERLY. WHAT SEEMS TO BE THE TROUBLE THIS MORNING?

WHAT'S WITH THE HANDKERCHIEF?

THAT'S WHAT I CAME TO TALK TO YOU ABOUT.

IF SOMEONE TRIED TO HURT YOU, YOU SHOULD GO TO THE POLICE.

THAT'S THE THING. I DON'T KNOW WHO ATTACKED ME.

JUST BETWEEN US, IF I WASN'T MISSING MY THUMB, I'D BE SURPRISED IF THEY'D BELIEVE MY STORY. I DON'T HAVE PROOF TO BACK IT UP.

THEN I STRONGLY URGE YOU TO VISIT MR. SHERLOCK HOLMES. HE HAS A WAY OF SOLVING UNSOLVABLE MYSTERIES.

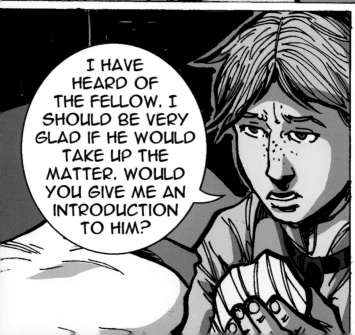

I HAVE HEARD OF THE FELLOW. I SHOULD BE VERY GLAD IF HE WOULD TAKE UP THE MATTER. WOULD YOU GIVE ME AN INTRODUCTION TO HIM?

I'LL DO BETTER. I'LL TAKE YOU ROUND TO HIM MYSELF.

DR. J. WATSON M.D.

IT IS EASY TO SEE THAT YOUR EXPERIENCE HAS BEEN NO COMMON ONE, MR. HATHERLY.

TELL US WHAT YOU CAN.

I AM AN ORPHAN AND A BACHELOR. I LIVE ALONE IN LONDON. BY DAY, I WORK AS A HYDRAULIC ENGINEER.

TWO YEARS AGO, I DECIDED TO GO INTO BUSINESS FOR MYSELF.

I RENT AN OFFICE ON VICTORIA STREET.

The day before…

ANY BUSINESS TODAY, HATHERLY?

NOPE. WHY WOULD WE EXPECT ANY DIFFERENT?

LOOK AT THOSE CUSTOMERS WALKING BY WITHOUT EVEN A GLANCE.

NOBODY WANTS WORK FROM US. WE'VE BEEN OPEN FOR TWO YEARS, AND WE'VE ONLY HAD THREE JOBS TOTAL.

WHAT HAVE WE GOT OURSELVES INTO? THE FEE IS AT LEAST TEN TIMES WHAT I WOULD HAVE ASKED FOR. AND IT'S POSSIBLE THAT THIS JOB MIGHT LEAD TO OTHER ONES.

ON THE OTHER HAND, I CAN'T THINK WHY I NEEDED TO COME SO LATE.

14

SOMEONE'S COMING!

WAIT!

I LEFT THIS DOOR SHUT JUST NOW.

SORRY. I WAS FEELING TRAPPED.

PERHAPS WE HAD BETTER PROCEED TO BUSINESS, THEN. MR. FERGUSON AND I WILL TAKE YOU UP TO SEE THE MACHINE.

DO YOU KNOW WHAT FULLER'S EARTH IS?

YES. I USE FULLER'S EARTH TO CLEAN MY HATS.

SOME TIME AGO, I BOUGHT A SMALL PLACE WITHIN TEN MILES OF READING. I DISCOVERED THAT THERE WAS A DEPOSIT OF FULLER'S EARTH IN ONE OF MY FIELDS.

I FOUND MY NEIGHBORS ON EITHER SIDE OF ME HAD MUCH LARGER DEPOSITS.

NATURALLY, I WANTED TO BUY THEIR LAND BEFORE THEY DISCOVERED ITS TRUE VALUE. BUT I HAD NO MONEY TO DO THIS. SO SOME FRIENDS AND I DECIDED TO SECRETLY WORK MY OWN LITTLE DEPOSIT TO EARN THE MONEY TO BUY THE NEIGHBORING FIELDS.

WE HAVE BEEN DOING THIS FOR SOME TIME. IN ORDER TO HELP US IN OUR OPERATIONS, WE BUILT A HYDRAULIC PRESS. THIS PRESS HAS GOTTEN OUT OF ORDER, AND WE WISH YOUR ADVICE UPON THE SUBJECT.

I QUITE FOLLOW YOU. BUT WHY DO YOU NEED A HYDRAULIC PRESS TO EXCAVATE FULLER'S EARTH? I THOUGHT IT WAS LIKE GRAVEL.

WE HAVE OUR OWN PROCESS.

WE PACK THE EARTH INTO BRICKS. THEN WE CAN TAKE IT OUT OF THE HOUSE WITHOUT ANYBODY KNOWING WHAT IT IS.

21

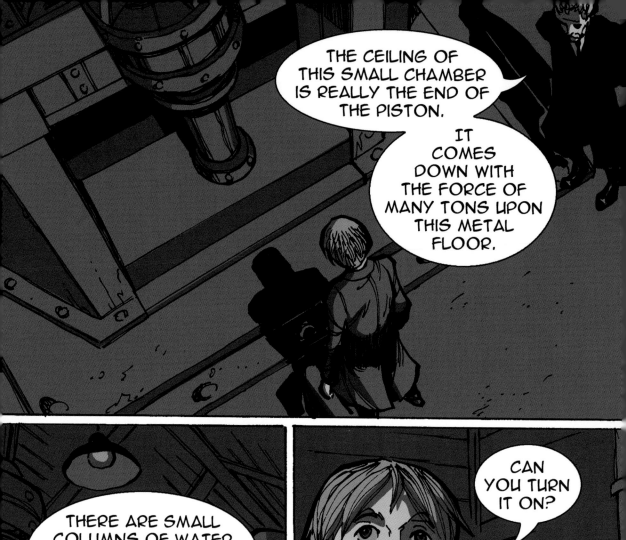

THE CEILING OF THIS SMALL CHAMBER IS REALLY THE END OF THE PISTON.

IT COMES DOWN WITH THE FORCE OF MANY TONS UPON THIS METAL FLOOR.

THERE ARE SMALL COLUMNS OF WATER OUTSIDE THAT RECEIVE AND TRANSMIT THE FORCE.

CAN YOU TURN IT ON?

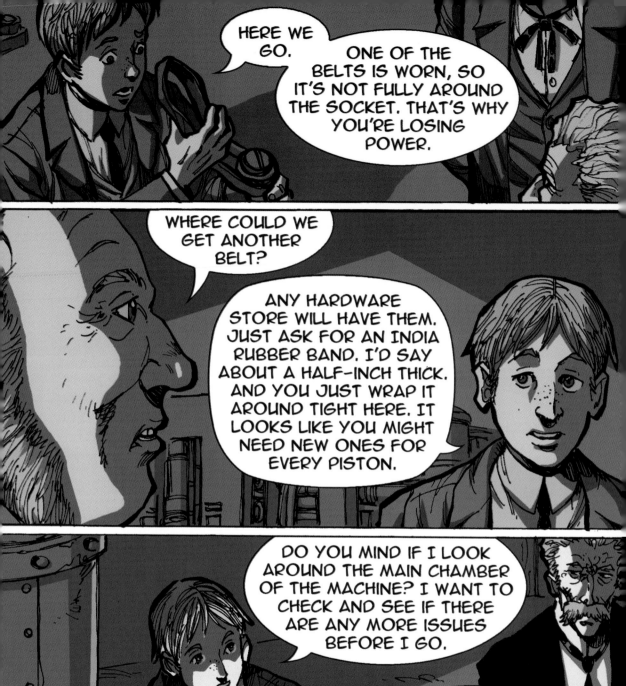

HERE WE GO.

ONE OF THE BELTS IS WORN, SO IT'S NOT FULLY AROUND THE SOCKET. THAT'S WHY YOU'RE LOSING POWER.

WHERE COULD WE GET ANOTHER BELT?

ANY HARDWARE STORE WILL HAVE THEM. JUST ASK FOR AN INDIA RUBBER BAND. I'D SAY ABOUT A HALF-INCH THICK. AND YOU JUST WRAP IT AROUND TIGHT HERE. IT LOOKS LIKE YOU MIGHT NEED NEW ONES FOR EVERY PISTON.

DO YOU MIND IF I LOOK AROUND THE MAIN CHAMBER OF THE MACHINE? I WANT TO CHECK AND SEE IF THERE ARE ANY MORE ISSUES BEFORE I GO.

YES, WONDERFUL. TAKE ALL THE TIME YOU NEED.

IT'S WOODEN HERE!

IT IS HIGH, BUT IT MAY BE THAT YOU CAN JUMP IT.

33

Three hours later…

WE'VE KNOWN FOR A WHILE ABOUT SOME COIN FORGERS IN THE AREA.

THEY HAVE BEEN TURNING OUT COUNTERFEIT COINS BY THE THOUSANDS.

WE EVEN TRACED THEM AS FAR AS READING, BUT COULD GET NO FARTHER. THEY COVERED THEIR TRACKS WELL.

BUT NOW, WE'VE CAUGHT A LUCKY BREAK.

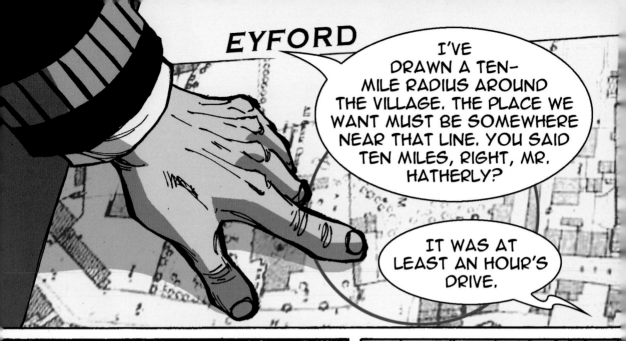

EYFORD

I'VE DRAWN A TEN-MILE RADIUS AROUND THE VILLAGE. THE PLACE WE WANT MUST BE SOMEWHERE NEAR THAT LINE. YOU SAID TEN MILES, RIGHT, MR. HATHERLY?

IT WAS AT LEAST AN HOUR'S DRIVE.

AND YOU THINK THAT THEY BROUGHT YOU BACK ALL THAT WAY WHEN YOU WERE UNCONSCIOUS?

SOMEBODY MUST HAVE. I FAINTED, AND THE NEXT THING I KNEW, I WAS IN THE VILLAGE.

WHAT I CANNOT UNDERSTAND IS WHY THEY WOULD LET YOU GO.

The End

HOW TO DRAW

SHERLOCK HOLMES

by BEN DUNN

STEP 1

Use a pencil to draw a simple framework. You can start with a stick figure! Then add circles, ovals, and cylinders to get the basic form. Getting the simple shapes in place is the beginning to solving any great case.

STEP 2

Time to add to Sherlock's look. Use the shapes you started with to fill in his clothes. Use guidelines to add circles for the eyes. And don't forget the hair.

STEP 3

Now you can go in with a pen and start inking Sherlock. Fill in all the details and fix any mistakes. Let the ink dry to avoid smudges, then erase any pencil marks. Sherlock is ready for some color, so grab your markers and get started!

GLOSSARY

accent a way of speaking a language that is usual for people of a certain area

bachelor a man who is not married

cleaver a large knife

convenient saving work or time; easy

counterfeit made to imitate something else in order to deceive

cylinder a solid figure of two parallel circles bound by a curved surface; a soda can is an example of a cylinder

deposit a collection of mineral matter in nature

deserted abandoned

discreet done quietly and secretly

essential very important or necessary

excavate to dig a hole

force a push or pull that causes an object to change its speed or the direction it's moving

forger someone who falsely makes or alters a document or object, such as a coin

fuller's earth earth that has mostly clay minerals and is used to absorb

guineas former coins used in the United Kingdom

hydraulic operated or moved by liquid

morose gloomy or angry

overhaul to repair thoroughly

piston a cylinder fit inside a hollow cylinder in which it moves back and forth; it is moved by or against fluid pressure in an engine

radius the distance from the center of a circle to any point along its edge

reference a statement of the qualifications of a person for a certain job given by someone who knows them

secrecy the condition of being hidden

sinister a person or thing that looks dangerous or evil

socket an opening that forms a holder for something

transmit to send or convey from one person or place to another

unconscious not being awake or aware of one's surroundings

unprofitable making no money

utmost greatest

ABOUT THE AUTHOR

Arthur Conan Doyle was born on May 22, 1859, in Edinburgh, Scotland. He was the second of Charles Altamont and Mary Foley Doyle's ten children. In 1868, Conan Doyle began his schooling in England. Eight years later, he returned to Scotland.

Upon his return, Doyle entered the University of Edinburgh's medical school, where he became a doctor in 1885. That year, he married Louisa Hawkins. Together they had two children.

While a medical student, Doyle was impressed when his professor observed the tiniest details of a patient's condition. Doyle later wrote stories where his most famous character, Sherlock Holmes, used this same technique to solve mysteries. Holmes first appeared in *A Study in Scarlet* in 1887 and was immediately popular.

Between 1887 and 1927, Doyle wrote 66 stories and 3 novels about Holmes. He also wrote other fiction and nonfiction novels throughout his life. In 1902, Doyle was knighted for his work in a field hospital in the South African War. Four years later, Louisa died. Doyle married Jean Leckie in 1907, and they had three children together.

Sir Arthur Conan Doyle died on July 7, 1930, in Sussex, England. Today, Doyle's famous character, Sherlock Holmes, is honored with societies around the world that pay tribute to the detective.

COLLECT THE

COMPLETE SERIES

ABOUT THE ADAPTERS

AUTHOR

Vincent Goodwin earned his B.A. in Drama and Communications from Trinity University in San Antonio. He is the writer of three plays as well as the cowriter of the comic book *Pirates vs. Ninjas II.* Goodwin is also an accomplished journalist, having won several awards for his work as a columnist and reporter.

ILLUSTRATOR

Ben Dunn founded Antarctic Press, one of the largest comic companies in the United States. His works appear in Marvel and Image comics. He is best known for his series *Ninja High School* and *Warrior Nun Areala.*